Paul Hutchens

D0596698

DISCARD

MOODY PUBLISHERS
CHICAGO

© 1950, 1998 by
PAULINE HUTCHENS WILSON

Revised Edition, 1998

All rights reserved. No part of this book may be repro-
duced in any form without permission in writing from the
publisher, except in the case of brief quotations embod-
ied in critical articles or reviews.

Original Title: *Sugar Creek Gang on the Mexican Border*

Cover Design: Ragont Design
Cover Illustration: Don Stewart

ISBN: 978-0-8024-7022-5
Printed by Bethany Press in Bloomington, MN – 12/13

We hope you enjoy this book from Moody Publishers.
Our goal is to provide high-quality, thought-provoking
books and products that connect truth to your real needs
and challenges. For more information on other books
and products written and produced from a biblical per-
spective, go to www.moodypublishers.com or write to:

Moody Publishers
820 N. LaSalle Boulevard
Chicago, IL 60610

7 9 10 8

Printed in the United States of America

PREFACE

Hi—from a member of the Sugar Creek Gang!

It's just that I don't know which one I am. When I was good, I was Little Jim. When I did bad things—well, sometimes I was Bill Collins or even mischievous Poetry.

You see, I am the daughter of Paul Hutchens, and I spent many an hour listening to him read his manuscript as far as he had written it that particular day. I went along to the north woods of Minnesota, to Colorado, and to the various other places he would go to find something different for the Gang to do.

Now the years have passed—more than fifty, actually. My father is in heaven, but the Gang goes on. All thirty-six books are still in print and now are being updated for today's readers with input from my five children, who also span the decades from the '50s to the '70s.

The real Sugar Creek is in Indiana, and my father and his six brothers were the original Gang. But the idea of the books and their ministry were and are the Lord's. It is He who keeps the Gang going.

PAULINE HUTCHENS WILSON

1

Long before we left Sugar Creek for our winter vacation along the Rio Grande River, I had been sure that when we went fishing down there we'd catch a fish as big as a boy.

I was *so* sure of it that I started telling nearly everybody I met about it. Why, that great big fish we were going to land might be as big as Little Jim, the smallest member of our gang, or maybe as big around as Poetry, the barrel-shaped member and the most mischievous one of us, who, because he wants to be a detective someday, is always getting us mixed up in some mysterious and exciting adventure.

But when, instead of a big fish, we caught something else just as big and had to pounce upon it and hold onto it for dear life or it would have gotten away—and also had to keep on holding on or we'd maybe have gotten our eyes scratched out or ourselves badly slashed up—well, I just couldn't have imagined anything so excitingly different happening to a gang of ordinary boys.

Of course, our gang wasn't exactly ordinary. Anyway, Circus, our acrobat and expert wrestler, wasn't. Big Jim, our fuzzy-mustached leader, wasn't either. Neither was Dragonfly, the pop-eyed member, who was always seeing exciting things first and also was always sneezing at the wrong time because he was allergic to nearly everything.

Certainly Little Jim, the smallest one of us, wasn't ordinary. He was an especially good boy, which any ordinary boy knows isn't exactly ordinary. He wasn't any sissy, though, as you'll see for yourself when I get to that part of the story where Little Jim joined in the struggle we were having with a very savage, wild, mad some-thing-or-other one moonlit night on the American side of the Rio Grande.

Even I myself, Bill Collins, red haired and freckle faced and a little bit fiery tempered part of the time, wasn't exactly ordinary. My mother says that most of the time I don't even act like what is called "normal"—whatever that is.

Well, here goes with the story of the Sugar Creek Gang along the Rio Grande.

The Rio Grande is a wet boundary between Mexico and the United States and is a long, wide, reddish-brown river that the people who live down at the bottom of Texas have har-nessed up and put to work for them—kind of the way Dad harnesses old Topsy, our mud-col-ored horse, and drives her around all over the Sugar Creek territory wherever he wants to.

The way they harnessed the river was by digging miles and miles of ditches for its water to flow all around through the Rio Grande Val-ley to irrigate their orange and lemon and grapefruit groves and patches where they grow cabbage and lettuce and carrots and other garden stuff. They also purify some of the water to make it safe for drinking and cooking.

Of course, a lot of interesting things happened to our gang before that last exciting night—but I'll just sort of skim over those so I can get to the most dangerous part in less than maybe a couple dozen pages. Soon I'll be galloping with you right through the—but you wait and see what.

"Maybe my dad will decide to buy a grapefruit grove down along the Rio Grande, and maybe we'll move down there to live," Dragonfly said to me sadly about two days before we left for Texas.

He had come over to my house to play with me that snowy morning, and he and I were out in the barn cracking black walnuts and gobbling up the kernels as fast as we could. Every now and then his face would get a messed-up expression on it, and he would sneeze, which meant he either had a cold or was allergic to something or other in our barn.

Hearing him say that didn't make me feel very happy. Even though he sometimes was sort of a nuisance to the gang, he'd been one of us as long as any of us had, and it would make a very sad hole in our gang if he left us for good.

"Daddy says we'll have to try out the climate first to see if we like it," he said, still sad in his voice and sad on his face. Then he added hopefully, "I hope I have to sneeze every five minutes after we get there."

"Why?" I asked.

"Because I'd rather live up here at Sugar Creek where I only have to sneeze every *seven* minutes"—which would have been funny if it hadn't been almost true.

Just that minute Mom's voice came quavering out across our cold, snowy barnyard the way it does when she is calling me to come to the house for a while for something. So in only a few jiffies, Dragonfly and I were both diving headfirst through the snow to our back door.

When we got inside the house, Dragonfly started sneezing again like a house afire, and it wasn't because of the good-smelling dinner Mom was cooking on our kitchen stove, either.

It was after we went into the living room, where Mom and Charlotte Ann, my baby sister, were that Dragonfly let out those stormy sneezes, six or seven of them in fast succession. Right away he exclaimed, "I smell somebody's powder!"

I quick looked at Mom's friendly, motherly face to see if her nose had any shine on it, the way it sometimes has when she's been working in the kitchen and hasn't remembered to powder it. It was a little bit shiny, so maybe Dragonfly was mistaken, I thought.

"The doctor says I'm allergic to some kinds of face powder," he said. He screwed up his face and sneezed three more times in even quicker succession than he had the other time. He looked with worried eyes first at Mom and then at Charlotte Ann.

My little sister, I noticed, was over in the corner, sitting on the floor. And she had Mom's face powder box open and some of the powder had spilled out, making it look as if somebody had scattered peach-colored dust over about three square feet of the rug.

Right away, Dragonfly and I were out of doors again, getting there quicker than our old Mixy-cat could have gone if Dragonfly's Airedale dog had been chasing her.

All of a sudden, I got what wasn't a very bright idea. "You don't *have* to stay down South if you don't want to," I said to him.

"Why?"

"If you can *really* sneeze a lot while you're there, your folks won't move down to stay, will they?"

"No, but what if I *can't*? I can only sneeze when I'm close to something I'm allergic to." He scooped up a double handful of snow, made a ball of it, whirled, and threw it across the barnyard through the fast-falling flakes toward Topsy, our old horse, who was standing on the east side of the barn with her tail to the wind, the way horses do if they're standing outdoors in a storm.

"Look," I said, "let me fix you up a little box of Mom's face powder. And when you get down there, you—well, you'll know what to do with it."

He looked at me with a sneezy expression on his face and said, "I couldn't fool Dad. Besides, my mother would smell the powder on me and wonder if I was turning into a girl or something. She might even be allergic to it herself. She says I inherited the sneezes from her."

I knew several other things Dragonfly had maybe inherited from her, such as believing it meant bad luck if a black cat crossed your path or if you broke a looking glass, and good luck if you found a horseshoe. He also had a hard time not believing in ghosts, even though he went to our church and had become a Christian one day when he was sliding down a sycamore tree along Sugar Creek, like Zaccheus in the Bible. Because his mother believed in ghosts—or almost did anyway—it made it hard for him not to.

Dragonfly had a nice mother though, but he being her only boy, she worried about him too much, and that worried *him*.

Well, even my dad got what Mom called the "warm climate bug," and because Mom hadn't had any vacation for years, they decided we'd take our car and drive down to the bottom of Texas, too. That meant that with *two* cars going, there'd be room in the backseats for six boys to go along—which is how many of us there are in our gang except for little Tom Till, the seventh one of us, who had to stay home and help take care of his mother. He also was going to help his father do the chores for us while my family was gone.

Before I go any farther, maybe I had better explain to you how in the world a gang of school-age boys could get to go on a great warm-climate vacation in the middle of winter. If I don't, nearly every mother who reads about us getting to go will wonder, *What on earth—*

and why? And some of them might even start to worry about us.

Well, it just so happened that a lot of coal miners in the United States, not even knowing how bad we all needed a vacation from school, went on what is called a "strike." They didn't work for so long that the schools around Sugar Creek got low on coal, and most of them had to close for a while.

You could have knocked us over with a snowflake when we found out that the Sugar Creek School was going to close, too. Of course, the school could have burned wood, but the school board decided not to do that, so we almost *had* to go on a vacation to show the coal miners how much we appreciated their not working.

My parents, especially Mom, felt sorry for the coal miners' wives, who might not have enough money to buy their groceries, and she hoped the miners' little children wouldn't have to go hungry.

Dad didn't say much except that coal mining was very hard work and any man who had to work all day in a mine, wearing out his muscles and sometimes his lungs away down under the earth, certainly ought to have good wages —as much as his boss could afford to pay.

But anyway, the coal miners' strike was good for the Sugar Creek Gang, for as soon as our school closed, we quick packed up, and away we went.

On the way to the Mexican border, we

stopped to see some interesting places, one of which was Turkey Run State Park. In the summertime it is one of the most beautiful places in the world, having deep canyons and gorges cut right through sandstone rock.

"We'll have to come here sometime in the summer," Dad said, "when old Sugar Creek isn't all chained with ice and snow."

"*Sugar* Creek!" Dragonfly exclaimed. "Is *that* Sugar Creek?"

"Sure," Poetry said. He was in the backseat of our car with Dragonfly and me. "Don't you know your geography?"

"What's geography got to do with Sugar Creek?" Dragonfly asked. He was not very good in that subject.

Poetry answered, "Don't you know that Sugar Creek is the very center of the geographical world? Anybody knows that!"

Sometimes Poetry used such an argumentative tone of voice that it made me want to talk back even when I agreed with him, but this time I didn't let myself. I said to Dragonfly, "Sure, anybody knows that"—which anybody does.

The next place we stopped was at one of my cousins' houses, not very far from Turkey Run. There we left Charlotte Ann so that the coal miners' strike would be good for Mom as well as for the rest of us. When Charlotte Ann's around and not asleep, there isn't a moment of peace for anybody. She is what is called a "normal" two-year-old girl, which means it is very hard on her nerves to have to be quiet.

As soon as Mom and Charlotte Ann had finished crying, we started on, and Dad drove a little faster to make up for lost time, which Mom said wasn't lost.

When we were going through Vincennes, Indiana, Dad reminded us that it was the first capital of what our history books call Indian Territory.

Then we crossed a big river to go into Illinois, and Dragonfly looked out and down at the water and said, "Old Sugar Creek's water certainly looks good this far from home."

"You're crazy," Poetry said. "That's the Wabash River."

"I know it," Dragonfly said, "but our geography book has a map in it that shows Sugar Creek emptying its water into the Wabash away back up there somewhere not far from Turkey Run, so some of that water down here is Sugar Creek water."

It kind of pleased me that Dragonfly was smart enough to think of that. And of course he was right. Some of the water in the Wabash River had been given to it absolutely free by good old Sugar Creek.

At a smallish town called Samburg in Tennessee, which we drove out of our way to go through the next day, Dad stopped while we looked at a terribly big lake and told us, "That's Reelfoot Lake, boys. It was made by an earthquake in 1811—supposed to be the biggest earthquake America ever had."

It certainly was the strangest-looking lake I

ever saw. It looked as if there were maybe ten thousand old tree stumps sticking up all over it. There were also a lot of whole trees, especially cypress, making it look like a forest growing in a lake. Part of it looked like a Sugar Creek cemetery with a lot of black ghosts standing around in it.

"That's probably some of Sugar Creek's water, too," Dragonfly said. "Let's go in swimming."

"Don't carry a good joke too far," Poetry said, scowling.

But Dad heard what Dragonfly had said. "You're right, Roy"—that being Dragonfly's civilized name. "At the time of the earthquake, the Mississippi River had something like an epileptic fit. Its water backed up and filled all the huge cracks and crevices which the earthquake had made. Some of that water was probably Sugar Creek water, because Sugar Creek flows into the Wabash and the Wabash into the Ohio and the Ohio into the Mississippi. Yes, that's probably partly Sugar Creek water."

All of a sudden Little Jim, who had been standing beside me, broke away, made a dash down to the lake, scooped up a double handful of water, and, with a grin on his mouselike face, tossed the water up in the air over our heads. A second later some of it spattered on my freckled face, while he yelled, "Hurrah, it's raining Sugar Creek water!"

It was time to drive on, so we did, not stopping at any place very important. And then we came to Houston, a big city in Texas, where there was a natural history museum and a zoo, called the Hermann Park Zoo.

2

It had been a long time since any of us had been to a zoo, and because most of us were tired almost to death of riding and wanted to take a walk, our two sets of parents drove us out to Hermann Park. There we walked around the grounds and saw a lot of wild animals and snakes and strange-looking birds. It was more fun than a barrel of monkeys to see everything —*especially* the different kinds of monkeys. There wasn't any snow on the ground here, so we walked around with our coats off like everyone else and felt as warm as if we were in the middle of a Sugar Creek summer. Dragonfly wasn't sneezing a bit and felt wonderful.

I noticed that lots of people were walking around looking at the different exhibits, but the thing I liked best, for a while anyway, was a very small lake with palm trees and a banana plant growing on a little island in the middle of it. All around the shore and on the island, big, ugly-looking alligators were sleeping in the sun.

That reminded Poetry of a poem, which he started to quote:

"Lazy bones, sleepin' in the sun,
How you 'specs to get your day's work done?"

Some of the alligators were sleeping only a few feet from us on the other side of a low fence, which they could have knocked down if they had wanted to. Maybe they would have if they had been hungry for fresh boy meat.

Circus yelled down at one that was about eight feet long and said, "Wake up, you lazy, good-for-nothing *mississippiensis!*"

"Wake up *what?*" Dragonfly wanted to know.

And Circus answered, "That is the scientific name for him."

Mississippiensis certainly was a terrible-looking animal. It had a very broad head with a rounded snout and was black all over except for some dull yellow markings the color of a boy's faded straw hat after it has been in the sun and wind for maybe five summers.

"How would you like to get a fish like that on your line when we go fishing down in the Gulf of Mexico?" Big Jim asked Little Jim.

That little guy looked up from where he was standing beside me and said, "That is no fish; that is a crocodilian reptile," which I happened to know it was, from a book I had in my library at home. "Besides," Little Jim added, "alligators don't live in the Gulf of Mexico but in swamps and rivers"—which I also knew, probably before Little Jim did.

"How about the Rio Grande River?" Poetry asked. "We might go fishing there too."

None of us knew for sure whether there were alligators in the Rio Grande. But I sort of hoped there wouldn't be, because a *wild* alligator might be hungrier than one that was sleeping in the Houston sun, acting the way my dad does sometimes when he has just had a chicken dinner and wants to take a nap and Mom wants him to help with the dishes and I get to help instead.

Right that second, Dragonfly started to get a messed-up expression on his face. He quick grabbed his nose, looked around worriedly, and sneezed in the direction of a pen of wolves and coyotes.

Circus looked toward the wolves, too, and let out a fierce, wild-sounding, high-pitched wail that was supposed to be like a wolf making a wolf call.

And that started things. In a second there was a wild hullabaloo of wolves' and coyotes' voices, howling and yelping and making a bloodcurdling chorus of cries.

Well, Hermann Park Zoo was certainly a very interesting place to visit, and it felt good to be walking around without our coats and hats. It made me feel sorry for all the people at Sugar Creek who had to live in cold weather.

That night when we were all in our motel cabins and I was in bed with Little Jim in another bed about four feet from mine, all of a sudden he started to mumble something in his sleep. I had been lying there looking out at a very bright moon, which was shining on me through a window, and listening to the rasping sound that the wind made blowing through the leaves of a palm tree. One of the palm's long, turkey-feather-shaped branches was brushing against the tiled roof of our cabin.

I strained my ears to hear what Little Jim might be dreaming about. He groaned as if he was having trouble of some kind. Then his bed-springs jiggled as though he was turning over, which he did with an impatient flip-flop, the way a boy does when something wakes him up too early in the morning and he doesn't want to get up. I heard him let out an extralong tired-out sigh, and then he was breathing a very regular noisy-boy kind of breathing, which meant he was asleep again.

Generally, not very much can wake me up once I drop off to sleep.

It had been such a wonderful trip so far, I thought. We'd seen so many things and had so much fun. Also, it seemed wonderful to be in a warm place right here in the United States. I got to thinking about all the wild animals I had seen in their cages, and I was glad the Sugar Creek Gang didn't have to live in cages but were as free as the red-winged blackbirds that make their nests along the Sugar Creek bank and whose songs are so pretty to listen to that it almost makes a boy's heart hurt to hear them.

Up above the telephone-pole-shaped palm tree outside, I could see—when the wind whipped the branches around just right—the whole big, round face of the moon, which right that same minute was also shining down on a lot of terribly cold snowdrifts and bare trees up

North and also on old frozen-faced Sugar Creek itself.

I drifted off into a strange sort of dream then. A big ugly, scaly, black alligator with straw-hat-colored markings on him raised his head up out of Sugar Creek, opened his mouth, and made a lunge for Little Jim, who was in swimming with the rest of us. It was a terrible dream, and I was still scared when I woke up. But Little Jim was there in his bed beside me, still sleeping, so right away I felt good again. Later, when I told Dad about my dream, he sort of laughed and said, "That is because you ate too big a supper."

It took us a day of driving to get from Houston to the Rio Grande Valley, that very pretty territory at the bottom of the United States map. But all of a sudden we were there, and our cars were flying along a road with palm trees and orange and lemon and grapefruit groves on each side.

Dragonfly and Poetry were in the backseat with me at the time. "Look," Dragonfly said, "there are a lot of people working out in the field."

"Migrant workers," my dad said from behind the steering wheel. "There are thousands of them working in the Rio Grande Valley between Brownsville and El Paso. People used to call them 'wetbacks.'"

"What's a wetback?" Dragonfly asked.

Dad, who always seemed to know something about everything because he was always reading and learning, said, "A wetback is a Mexican who has entered our country illegally by wading or swimming across the Rio Grande. They get jobs here and make a lot more money than they can in their own country. Some of them go back to Mexico later, where they spend the money."

Poetry and Dragonfly and I got interested in something else just then, while Mom and Dad talked about different things. I didn't realize what kind of things until I heard Dad say, "They found thirty-eight dead illegal immigrants in the Rio Grande in one year."

Mom gasped, and I sat up straight to listen, especially since Poetry's elbow pushed itself against my ribs and he raised a mysterious finger to his lips.

But I spoke up quick and said to Dad, "What's that?"

"Oh, nothing," Mom said, not wanting me to hear anything she called "gruesome" and not remembering that I wasn't little anymore.

"Did they drown trying to swim across?" Dragonfly asked. He *was* maybe too little to hear about such things.

Dad must have decided we could stand it, so he said, "They were murdered."

"Murdered!" Mom exclaimed, and the way she said it made me think maybe she was too little herself.

"It's this way," Dad explained. "After an illegal immigrant has been in our country long enough to have a nice little sum of money, he tries to go back secretly, sometimes swimming or wading or being rowed across the river. Evidently some criminals were hiding out along the river, watching for any illegals who were going home. They waylaid them at the border either on the Texas or the Mexico side, robbed and killed them, and threw their bodies into the river."

"How did they kill them?" Dragonfly asked.

"In different ways," Dad said and changed the subject. "Look, here's where we turn off to go to McAllen. This road goes on to Brownsville."

Dad slowed down, turned right, and away we went west on a road that was numbered Routes 83 and 281. We went zipping along between orange and grapefruit orchards. Tall palm trees were on either side of the road the way maples and elms border the roads back home. Our car window was open, and the cool, friendly breeze that came in felt wonderful on my warm freckled face.

The towns seemed so close together that you were in the middle of the next one almost before you left the end of the last—towns such as Mercedes, Welasco, Donna, and Pharr. And then in a little while we were in McAllen, where I noticed that most of the people were Mexicans. They had dark hair, and everybody was busy and looked happy, and the stores were nearly all new.

Dad drove straight to a hotel, which was named Casa de Palmas. That means "House of

Palms." He and Mom and Dragonfly's parents went in to register, while we six boys climbed out of the cars. We roamed around kind of bashfully, looking at different things, especially the big palm trees and the red double-sized poinsettias blossoming at the tops of flower stalks higher than our heads. We also looked at a beautiful vine with brilliant purplish-red flowers, which Little Jim, who had a book of garden flowers at home, said was bougainvillea.

Circus didn't seem very happy. He had a dark scowl on his face, so I said, "'S'matter, Circus?"

He said gloomily, "Who wants to climb a palm tree?"

As you know, Circus would rather climb a tree than do anything else, and if ever we don't know where he is at Sugar Creek, we always look *up* when we try to find him.

"Yeah," Poetry said, being so chubby he couldn't climb one anyway. "Who does?"

We were standing right beside a palm whose smooth, gray trunk zoomed straight up almost forty feet before there were any limbs. In fact, there weren't any limbs at all but only a lot of dark green fan-shaped leaves as big as an elephant's ears in the Hermann Park Zoo. Circus was right, I thought. A palm tree might be very pretty to look at, but no tree seemed like a good tree to a boy if he couldn't climb it or swing on its branches or pick mulberries or cherries or something from it. And you couldn't do any of that to the prettiest, straightest palm tree in the world.

Dragonfly's dad and my dad arranged for all of us six boys to sleep in an apartment over somebody's garage away out at the edge of town, not far from what is called the "brush." That's the name of the thick forestlike woods that grow all along the Rio Grande River. The garage and apartment belonged to a man who had lived at Sugar Creek a long time ago before any of our gang was born. He had been a special friend of Dragonfly's parents and had been trying to get them to move down there. They had fixed up enough beds for all of the gang to sleep.

Mom didn't exactly want to stay in the fancy hotel that Dad had picked out for her, but Dad had decided she had to. "You're going to live in luxury and be waited on and not have to cook a single meal or wash a dish for a whole week," he'd said.

Even before we had left home, Dad told me about it, saying, "It's this way, Son. A man who really loves his wife ought to see to it that she gets a little variety in life, even if it seems to cost a lot of money, because a wife is worth more than the money it costs to take care of her. There is nothing a man can buy that is more important than his wife's goodwill and good health. And your mother needs a vacation pretty badly—a lot more than she thinks she does. She has worked very hard all these years, and I can tell it is beginning to get on her nerves. We have a pretty wonderful wife and mother, Bill —you know that, don't you?"

He and I had been out in the barn at the time, and Mom had just called us to supper. I had known she was that kind of a mother all my life without anybody having to tell me. But when Dad said that, I looked up at his big bushy eyebrows and his gray-green eyes under them, and I think maybe for the first time I realized that Mom belonged to both of us. It was up to us to look after her, and take care of her, and not let her work too hard, and to see to it that she didn't have too much to worry about. Also it seemed maybe I ought to try to be a better boy than I had been.

"Sure," I said to Dad, and that evening when I had gone up to the haymow to throw down hay for old Topsy and the cows, I stayed up there a little longer than I sometimes do. As you maybe know, away off in a far corner of our haymow where there is a crack between the logs, I had a very special place in the hay where sometimes, when I felt lonesome and also when I was especially happy inside, I liked to go. I would take out from the crack in the logs my little brown leather New Testament, which I kept there, and would read a verse or two or more. Then I'd drop down on both knees in the hay and pray something to God, whom I liked even better than I liked my folks and who had made all the world we lived in and had sent His Son to be our Savior.

I can't remember exactly what I prayed that

late afternoon, but there was sort of an ache in my heart because maybe I had caused my mother too much worry that summer and winter. So I asked God to help me to do something about myself, to make me kinder to my mother, and also to help me actually look for things I could do to help her around the house and yard without being told to. I felt I wanted to be as kind to her as Dad was.

3

Well, there we were in the Rio Grande Valley, all six of the Sugar Creek Gang and four of our parents, and I just knew something absolutely very, very different was going to happen to us. We were going fishing in the Gulf of Mexico and visit Old Point Lighthouse at Port Isabel. Also we were going to cross over the Rio Grande to Old Mexico and see different things there. Why, we might run into some kind of a dangerous experience with an illegal immigrant or a criminal of some kind.

That night when the gang was sitting and lying and sprawling around on bunks and chairs and gliders on our upstairs apartment porch, chattering about our trip and the wonderful warm weather and planning tomorrow's adventures, Poetry was on the glider beside me helping me make it swing. He sort of leaned his head over next to my shoulder and whispered, saying, "If we expect to really have an exciting adventure down here, we may have to go out and look for one. Adventures are funny things. They don't come hunting you up—you have to go where they happen."

I was kind of sleepy and not too interested in having any kind of adventure right that minute. Certainly I didn't want to start out that night in a new place like Texas, especially when our apartment wasn't too far from a regular jungle of strange trees, bushes, prickly pear cactus, which is called "cat's claw," and mesquite, and stuff. It was the kind of growth you have to watch out for all the time when you walk through it, or you'll get scratched or stuck or clawed. Definitely I didn't want to look for any adventures in the dangerous dark, which it probably would be, that close to the Mexican border.

So I grunted and answered Poetry, saying, "Let's all get to bed so we'll feel like a million dollars in the morning and be ready for our trip into Old Mexico."

"Sh!" Poetry said. "Don't mention money out here on this open porch. You remember they throw dead bodies in the Rio Grande River after they have robbed and killed them."

"They just do that to illegals," I said.

Little Jim heard me say that and spoke up and said, "What's an illegal?"

I remembered then that Little Jim had not been in the car with us when we had talked about them. So pretty soon all of us were discussing illegal immigrants. I explained to Little Jim and the others that they are Mexican citizens who, because they can make more money working in the United States or maybe because they don't have any work in their hometowns, wade or swim or maybe row across the Rio Grande to get a job here.

"Why don't they just go right down to the bridge and *walk* across?" Little Jim asked.

"Because they aren't supposed to work in the United States unless they are American citizens," Big Jim said, "which you aren't if you are born in Mexico. If the United States let all of the Mexicans who wanted to come over here, there wouldn't be any jobs left for the people who are already citizens. And maybe the Mexicans would work all summer and make a lot of money and just take it all back to Mexico and spend it there instead of here in our country."

I didn't understand it very well myself. It sounded like some things we were supposed to study in our history and civics books in school, and I wasn't very good in those subjects. But I remembered what Dad had said in the car that afternoon, so I kept on explaining it.

"Sometimes when they try to go back across the river at night, robbers waylay them and take their money. Sometimes they kill them and throw their bodies in the Rio Grande. One year the police found thirty-eight different bodies of people who—" That was as far as I got.

Big Jim interrupted me then. "Let's don't talk about stuff like that before going to bed, or somebody will have a nightmare."

Well, if there is anything I don't like more than I don't like anything else it is to be shushed right in the middle of something I am saying, so I said to Big Jim, "Oh, of course, if you're scared or nervous or—"

Then Big Jim shushed me again and said, "Listen, everybody. Somebody's singing or something."

So I shushed myself and listened, expecting to hear some pretty Mexican music, but instead it was a quartet of men's voices singing a very cheerful gospel song, which we sometimes sing on Sunday in the Sugar Creek church. It was:

"I won't have to cross Jordan alone—
Jesus died for my sins to atone."

"It's a sound truck," Big Jim said. "It's coming nearer"—which it was.

Because every single one of the Sugar Creek Gang liked to hear gospel songs and hymns, we all kept still and listened. As quick as the quartet finished, I heard a loud, amplified voice say:

"Beginning Sunday night in the big tent on the highway between Donna and Pharr, be sure to hear the Rio Grande quartet and the boy evangelist David Mulder. Everyone is invited. See also the Christian motion picture *Dust or Destiny*. Admission free."

All of a sudden I got a warm feeling in my heart. My folks had taken me to church ever since I was old enough to be carried there, and I was glad the people way down here, halfway to the bottom of the world, were going to hear the gospel, too. I had never heard a "boy preacher," and I wished the gang could get to go tomorrow night to hear him.

Also, I would like to see an honest-to-goodness Christian movie in a big tent. None of the Collins family ever went to the Sugar Creek theater, because Dad and Mom both have told me so many times I can quote it from memory, "The motion picture industry as a whole is rotten, Bill, and even though there may be a good picture once in a while, we do not believe we should support it." Also our minister says that people who go to shows all the time never care very much about getting anybody to become a Christian. So if I got to see an honest-to-goodness *Christian* picture, it would be fine.

The sound of the sound truck faded away as it went on down the street.

"What's the Jordan?" Dragonfly asked all of a sudden, as if he had just that second heard the quartet singing "I Won't Have to Cross Jordan Alone."

Poetry said, "That's the name of a river in Palestine."

"Was somebody afraid he would have to go across all by himself?" Dragonfly asked, being slower even than I am to understand things like that.

All of us were quiet for a while. Even though every single one of us liked to listen to other people talk about things the Bible teaches, still we were kind of bashful about doing it ourselves. But I knew that if our minister had been with us and Dragonfly had asked that question, he'd probably have said, "In the song, 'the Jordan' means death. The man who wrote it meant that, when he died, the Savior would meet him on the bank of the river of death and go across with him."

In fact, Big Jim himself said that very thing a minute later.

Then Dragonfly asked an ignorant question that got me started thinking about the Rio Grande and illegals again. "When we die, will we wade across or swim across or will there be a boat or a canoe?"

Even Little Jim knew better than to ask a dumb question like that. He piped up right then in his small friendly voice and said, "It's not an actual *river!*"—which anybody knows it isn't.

Anyway, it was time for us all to get into our nightclothes and also into our bunks. I was so sleepy by that time that I was sure, if my eyes ever went shut without my knowing it, it would be morning before I opened them again.

But right after I had finished saying a quiet good-night prayer and just as Poetry finished his, he and I slipped out onto the moonlit porch again. The weather was so warm that we could be out there in our pajamas without even feeling chilly. I noticed that the moon's round face was as clean and white as it had been in Houston last night. It seemed wonderful to think that right below us on the lawn was an honest-to-goodness orange tree with honest-to-goodness oranges on it. Tomorrow maybe we could pick one apiece and eat them.

A warm breeze was blowing, and the extra-long branches of the palm tree in the center of the lawn swung from side to side, making a very happy swishing sound as they rubbed together. It was like the sound the waves of a lake make, washing and washing against a sandy shore.

I had heard that same friendly over-and-over-again sound many a summer moonlit night on vacations the gang had taken in northern Minnesota, which I have told you about in some of the other Sugar Creek Gang books.

All of a sudden Poetry said, "Listen."

I listened but couldn't hear anything except the wind. "It's the wind in the palm tree," I said.

And he said, "I know it."

Because nearly everything Poetry ever saw or heard or tasted or smelled or felt reminded him of a poem, he started quoting part of one we had all memorized from one of our Sugar Creek schoolbooks. It went something like this:

> The husky, rusty rustle
> Of tassels of the corn . . .

For the first time in my life I realized that whoever wrote that poem had made a mistake. Anybody who knows anything about a cornfield knows it isn't the *tassels* of the corn that make the rustling sounds in the wind, because they are too far apart to rub against each other.

But it is the big, long, sword-shaped *blades* brushing against each other that make the noise.

So I said to Poetry, "If James Whitcomb Riley had lived down here, he could have said, 'The husky, rusty rasping of the palm leaves of the palm'—or something."

Just thinking about the tall, dark-green grown-up corn that lives in the fields up North in the summer, and also thinking about the woods where maple, elm, ash, walnut, linden, and all kinds of other friendly trees grow, the kind a boy can climb and have fun in, made me lonesome for home. It didn't seem right for it to be summer weather in the winter.

But the moon looked just the way it did back home, and also it felt the same way to be sleepy down along the Rio Grande as it did along Sugar Creek. So Poetry and I left the moon to take care of itself and went inside, where most of the rest of us were asleep already.

In what seemed like only minutes, it was morning again, our first morning in the Rio Grande Valley. Right in the middle of the kind of noise a gang of boys makes when it starts waking up and getting up, I heard a bird outside making a very friendly, cheerful bird call. "Cheo. Cheo. Cheo . . ."

Little Jim, who was already up and out on the porch, called back in to us, "Hey, you guys, it's a cardinal!"

In a jiffy I was out there with him with only

one shoe on and still wearing my green-striped pajamas. I got there just in time to see what looked like a flash of red fire in the top of the orange tree before it shot like an arrow right through the warm blue-skied weather straight toward some other kind of tree in the direction of the brush, which was also in the direction of the Rio Grande River.

"If a cardinal flies across the river into Mexico, will somebody make him fly back again and live here?" Dragonfly asked.

Circus heard him say that and answered, "Birds don't have any nationality. They just belong to the world."

"Where do we eat?" Poetry wanted to know, and so did the rest of us.

Big Jim had a map of the town, so pretty soon we were on our way to the hotel, where we were supposed to meet the four parents, who were our chaperons while we were down there.

While we were half walking and half running beside and behind and in front of one another through the very interesting townful of Americans and Mexicans, I thought how much Mexicans just seemed like suntanned white people, except that they had the kind of a tan that would not have to have sunshine all the time or it would fade.

Then I was remembering Mom's last words to me yesterday when I had told her good night at the hotel before the gang left for our apartment: "Be a good boy, Bill—like you sometimes are when you don't have a chaperon."

There had been a twinkle in her eye, which meant she liked me but didn't quite trust me 100 per cent.

"What's a chaperon?" Dragonfly had asked.

And Poetry, trying to be funny, answered for me, saying, "It's what the rest of us are glad we don't have two apiece of."

When we got to the hotel desk, I asked the clerk to phone the room of Mr. and Mrs. Theodore Collins of Sugar Creek to tell them there were six boys in the lobby.

The friendly, middle-aged woman who was the telephone operator pressed a buzzer, waited for Dad or Mom to answer, and said, "There are six hungry boys waiting for you in the lobby."

"*Terribly* hungry," Poetry said.

"*Terribly* hungry," the middle-aged woman repeated into the telephone.

And Poetry's face turned as red as the red side of a maiden blush apple from the tree in his backyard at home.

"They will be down in about ten minutes," the telephone operator said. "You are to wait outside in the patio."

"Would you please call Dragonfly's parents too?" I asked, and the woman's mischievous eyes flashed from one to the other of our kind of homely faces as though she had never seen such different-looking faces in her life.

Maybe she hadn't, and she hadn't missed much either. There was Big Jim's face, which was the oldest-looking one with an almost mustache on his upper lip. Circus's face looked like one of the chimpanzees in the Hermann Park Zoo at Houston. Poetry's face looked like a full moon with a fat nose in the middle and with eyebrows that grew together in the center, just above the bridge of his nose. Dragonfly's face had a crooked nose, which he could see the south end of without looking in the mirror if he would shut his right eye. Little Jim's friendly, innocent face was mouse shaped. And finally there was mine with its very ordinary nose, which even in the winter had a lot of unnecessary freckles on it.

"Are you Dragonfly?" the telephone operator asked, looking straight at Dragonfly himself.

He grinned with a scowl on his forehead and answered, "Yes, ma'am," and swallowed as if he had a big lump in his throat.

"Your chaperons' names are Mr. and Mrs. Gilbert, aren't they?"

Pretty soon, while we were still waiting for the Gilbert and Collins parents, the gang was walking around on one of the hotel patios. It was like a large lawn with lawn furniture and colored outdoor umbrellas. But, where the grass was supposed to be, there was beautifully designed tiled flooring like the kind Poetry's parents had in the recreation room in the basement of their house.

"Look," Little Jim said, "yonder is a whole lot of live fishing poles."

We all looked where he was pointing. And,

sure enough, at the farther end of the tiled patio, on the back side of what looked like the latticed backdrop of a stage, was a cluster of maybe thirty tall, green bamboo stalks, most of them just the right size for fishing poles.

There were a lot of flowers and trees and shrubs on a pretty lawn on the other side of the hotel. And across the paved street in a park, which had a bandstand in the middle, there were many more flowers such as oleander, bougainvillea, roses, and poinsettias.

"Look," Circus said, "there are a lot of *melons* growing on that tree."

They weren't melons. They only looked like it, and we found out later they were called papaya. About fifteen of the green-and-orange fruits were hanging in a large cluster about eight feet from the ground.

Pretty soon Dad came out onto the patio.

Boy oh boy! Whew! Land sakes! I thought. Who was that tall woman in the extrapretty summer suit walking along with her hand resting in the crook of his arm? It couldn't be, it just *couldn't* be, and yet it *had* to be because it was! It was my very own mom dressed up in a brand-new toast-colored suit with a daffodil-colored blouse and a frilly collar, which had a neck shaped like the letter V. Also she was wearing a new perky hat with flowers on it, which made her look even more than ever special. She was wearing high-heeled green shoes too.

4

I stood stock-still and stared at my different-looking mother. She didn't even look as big around as she did at home. For a half second I couldn't believe it was her. Then Dragonfly beside me sneezed, and I remembered he was allergic to Mom's new face powder. Then my mixed-up mind found my lost voice, and I said, "How do you do, parents!"

Dad himself looked dressed up. He had on a noisy necktie that had a hand-painted tall palm tree on it with a pretty green lake in the background and a sailboat in the middle of the lake.

"The name is Collins," Dad said in a mischievous, dignified voice. "Mr. and Mrs. Theodore Collins of Sugar Creek." He held out his hand as if he was meeting me for the first time in my life.

Not to be outdone by him, I took his hand and shook it and also Mrs. Collins's hand.

Even if I hadn't seen Mom or heard her Sugar Creek voice, I would have known her just by looking at and feeling her hand. It was one of the same hands she used when she did the work at home, such as peeling potatoes or washing dishes while I dried them. It was also the same hand she had used to stroke my forehead once that very same winter when I had been sick with a high fever and she sat beside me the way she always does when I have to go to bed with a cold or something. It was also the same hand that, a couple of times or more, had given me a few sad spankings.

Pretty soon all of us were in the hotel's ritzy dining room waiting for breakfast.

"Quite a nice change," Mom said to Dragonfly's mom, when we were all seated around a large table. "It feels good to be waited on for once."

Dad heard her say that and caught my eye, and I could tell by the way he winked at me that he was feeling good that he and I could give Mom a winter vacation away from home with nothing for her to do.

All ten of us were seated at one big table at the end of the classy dining room and were waiting to be waited on by two white-coated Mexican boys.

I put on my mom's favorite table manners, which she had made for me herself. Because most of the rest of the gang were half scared or half bashful or both, we behaved the way all our parents thought we should.

With so many people all around us, I wondered what Dad would do about the blessing before we ate. I knew that if he asked it out loud, other people in the dining room might stop and look and listen as if we were some kind of odd people—which people do when you bow your head to pray in a public eating place, because most people start right in eating without praying, like cows do—cows not knowing any better, Dad says.

Pretty soon ten platters of buckwheat pancakes came steaming in. They were a pretty sight to see, not only when you looked around the table at them but also when you saw them reflected in the very large six-by-eight-foot mirror that was on the wall across from where I sat.

While I was still watching us in the mirror and while the two white-coated Mexican boys hurried back and forth around us, I noticed that Mom's green hat was the same color as the six or seven philodendron plants that were growing in the same number of copper flower pots on the branches of an iron tree standing in front of the mirror. I thought the color of the hat and the philodendron plant leaves was the same as a maple leaf in the woods back home. In the mirror I could even recognize the back of Mom's green hat and her head.

Just then Dad said to all of us, "Let's each one ask his own blessing quietly." Then he bowed his head first, and right away we all did the same thing. In a jiffy our ten quiet prayers were finished, and we were all sawing away on our pancakes.

Dragonfly's mom seemed even more bashful than she thought *he* was, because the Gilbert family hardly ever ate any meals anywhere except at home. I noticed that she kept watching her boy with a worried look on her face as if to see if he was using good manners. If he wasn't, it might mean she was to blame.

But Dragonfly was perfect. He had to sneeze only once, which he did very politely into his handkerchief while he turned his face to one side as if he was used to it, and he said, "Excuse me, please," which we all did without saying so.

"There was a time," Dad said to Dragonfly's dad across the corner of the table, "when I hesitated about bowing my head over my plate in a public dining room for fear of what people would think. But I don't feel that way about it anymore. I always begin my silent prayer by saying, 'May somebody with a heavy heart see me and be reminded that there is a God who loves him and to whom he can tell his troubles.'"

It was certainly different eating breakfast in that fancy dining room with all the windows wide open and the cool breeze blowing in and birds singing outside. But the gang didn't seem to be enjoying it as much as our chaperons were. We were eager to get started on some kind of an adventure where we could use our muscles to save somebody from danger or something.

Dad and Dragonfly's dad had already decided to spend part of their morning looking at citrus groves. Mom and Dragonfly's mom were going to "meander around the stores awhile," as Mom expressed it. We, the gang, could do anything we wanted to but had to be ready to meet at the hotel at 11:00. Then we would all drive across the Rio Grande to Old Mexico and maybe have dinner in a Mexican cafe. Also I hoped we would run into an honest-to-goodness adventure.

We stumbled onto the beginning of a different kind of adventure that very afternoon. We had been in Mexico for maybe an hour, driving and walking around and looking at the different interesting and educational things such as a very pretty, block-square, flower-filled, tree-shaded park, right in the middle of the town. We saw also a very gruesome-looking cemetery. The graves were only a couple of feet apart, and each of them had a black wooden cross for a marker and a wreath of dead or dying flowers hanging across the upright of the cross. There was a new cemetery right beside the older one, which had a sign in Spanish above the gate. Big Jim translated it for us, and it was "Modern Funerals, Day or Night."

Also our two lady chaperons visited what they called "exciting shops" and acted like two grown-up schoolgirls who were having the time of their lives looking at things and also buying stuff such as two baskets, a couple of scarves, and some fancy drinking glasses.

After our Mexican dinner and before going back across the border, Mom and Dragonfly's mom decided they wanted to look around in other exciting shops near the park, so Dad and Dragonfly's dad drove round and round looking for a place to park but couldn't find one until we came to an old Mexican church.

The very second we stopped and started to pile out, a bright-eyed, sincere-looking Mexican boy about my size came hurrying up, saying, "Watch your car—five cents," only it sounded like "Wash your car."

Dad looked at the boy with his bushy-eyebrow-shaded eyes, smiled at him from under his reddish-brown mustache, and said, "Sure," and handed him a whole quarter.

"*Muchas gracias, senor.* Thank you!" the boy said politely.

Our two mothers hurried across to the exciting shops while our two dads went to wait for them on one of the park benches.

That left the gang alone for a while, which we would rather be anyway. We looked at the store windows for a while and finally went into an interesting-looking saddle shop. When we came out into the bright sunshine where our car was, Dad and Mom and Dragonfly's mom and dad were just coming across the street from the park.

"Where's the boy I gave the quarter to?" Dad said, looking all around while we all started to do the same thing.

But do you know what? That black-haired, brown-skinned, friendly Mexican boy had disappeared.

Dad laughed a little, then said, "Maybe he ran off somewhere to spend his quarter."

In a few minutes we would be on our way to the bridge that spans the Rio Grande and soon would be back in the United States. Dragonfly's mom had bought a colored basket, so his dad put it in the trunk of their car and locked it. I remembered that the lock on the trunk of our car had been broken back home when Mom had been accidentally driving backward one day—and we hadn't had a chance to get the lock fixed before coming South.

At the river we were stopped by some officers who were stopping all cars because it was a toll bridge, and we had to pay a few cents apiece to ride across it.

Also, we had to answer different questions. Dragonfly and his parents and Big Jim and Circus were in the car ahead of ours. They got past Customs OK, and then came our turn.

"Are you all American citizens?" the officer asked us, and Poetry and I answered, "Yes."

He gave us all a quick lookover, winked at Poetry and Little Jim and me in the backseat, and said to Mom and Dad in the front seat, "Did you buy anything in Mexico valued at more than one hundred dollars?"

"Only a few useless trinkets," Dad said mischievously, and Mom held up some things she had in her lap.

"Anything in the trunk of your car?"

And that is where we had the beginning of our adventure.

5

Poetry and I got out to show the man there wasn't anything in our trunk—as Big Jim and Circus had done just ahead of us. I knew they had found Dragonfly's mom's new basket in their trunk.

Well, I guess I'd never had such a different kind of surprise in my life as when I lifted up our trunk with its smashed lock. I knew there was an old blanket in it, which we had used to cover some of our luggage when we drove down to the Rio Grande Valley to keep the dust off it, but that was all. Only it *wasn't*. There was something else covered up under the robe, and it was *alive!* I knew, because I saw it move. In fact, right that second I saw the five brown, bare toes of a boy's bare foot, just before it disappeared under the edge of the blanket.

The officer saw it, too, and yanked off the blanket. And what to my wondering eyes should appear but a boy, who was the owner of the five bare toes. It was Dad's twenty-five-cent Mexican boy, whom we had last seen in front of the church. He was all curled up in as small a ball as he could curl himself into.

Right away the officer started saying something in Spanish, and the boy started talking back to him in a worried, tearful voice. It sounded like a one-sided argument, and because the boy was the littlest of the two I felt sorry for him and wished I could understand Spanish so I could take his part and explain to the officer that whatever he was doing wasn't very bad.

Dragonfly's car was still waiting for ours, so in a flash Big Jim and Dragonfly and Circus came tumbling out and back to see what our noisy excitement was all about. Then our two dads came, a little slower, and for a minute all of us were standing in a mixed-up circle, looking into the trunk at the scared Mexican boy, who had an expression on his face like that of a small stray dog that nobody wanted.

It hurt my heart like everything to have to go on across the bridge and leave that cute-looking boy on his side of the Rio Grande. But the Mexican government couldn't let a boy do a thing like that, Dad explained to us. The boy wouldn't have anyone to look after him in Texas, and the state would have to feed him.

"Maybe he already has part of his parents in Texas," Little Jim said as we left the bridge and the brown river behind us.

In my mind's eye I could still see the tears in the boy's eyes. I felt so sorry for him I wished we could have put him right in the car with us and taken him across, but we couldn't.

That night, to my absolutely astonished surprise, we saw Dad's twenty-five-cent boy again.

The whole gang of us and our four chaperons went to church in the big, brown tent to hear the quartet and the boy evangelist. That was the most interesting meeting! It was just like one we had one summer in a large tent back home when some of our Sugar Creek Gang had been saved.

That was the time, as you maybe remember, when Circus's alcoholic dad started the Christian life, too. He had been sitting outside the tent in the dark, watching and listening, and when he saw his boy, Circus, go hurrying down the long grassy aisle to the platform to receive the Savior, it had melted his hard, cold heart. He had quickly ducked under the tent's side wall, scrambled in and onto his feet, still half drunk, and staggered down the aisle, crying out loud as he went, "That's my boy! That's my boy!"

That wonderful night, he and Circus and most of us and a lot of other people went into what is called an inquiry room beside the platform, where all of us had prayed on our knees in the long, mashed-down, brown grass. That had been the beginning of a new life for the whole Brown family—Brown is Circus's last name. After that, almost right away Circus's dad got a good job and started making a decent living for his large family of all girls except for one boy.

The boy evangelist's tent was nearly filled with different kinds of people. A lot of them were dressed in their working clothes, and nobody seemed to care. Mexicans—or Latin Americans, as Dad called them—and ordinary

Americans and maybe even some illegals were all more or less mixed up in the different sections.

It felt good to hear everybody singing the same songs and choruses we used in our own church. Some of the numbers were sung in Spanish and some in English. Part of one chorus, which the black-haired Mexican children on the front rows almost yelled their heads off on, was:

Hay perdon por la sangre de Jesus,
Hay perdon por su muerte in la crus—

When they translated it for us, I found it meant:

There is pardon by the blood of Jesus,
There is pardon by His death on the cross—

I liked the song right away, and in only a few minutes all the gang—who were sitting in two rows, behind and in front of each other away off to one side near one of the tent's side walls—were singing like a house afire along with the rest of the people

It seemed the Mexicans enjoyed singing it even better than we did, especially the children. They worked as hard singing as a gang of boys dashing *lickety-sizzle* through the woods to see which one could get to the swimming hole first.

But it certainly seemed different to hear a

boy not more than eleven or twelve years old preach to a tentful of people, quoting dozens of Bible verses, not having to stop to think what to say next, and every now and then slamming home something important. It was like a boy taking a fierce, hard swing at a hard-pitched baseball and hitting it and knocking a home run and all the people thinking it was grand and yelling for him—except that the tentful of different kinds of people didn't yell or shout.

But when the boy preacher said something extraimportant, several of the ministers who were sitting on the platform behind him would say, "Amen." Also, a number of the people who were sitting around us did the same thing kind of quietly. "Amen," as you maybe know, means "That's right" or "That's what I think too." It almost means about the same as saying "Attaboy," only it is more reverent.

It was when the quartet was singing the same song we had heard last night coming from the sound truck that my curiosity made me look around the tent to see what different people might be thinking. And that was when I saw the little twenty-five-cent boy we had found hidden in the trunk of our car!

When I first glimpsed him, he was crawling in under the tent's side wall. A second later he was on the edge of a bench beside a Mexican with a mustache. I noticed the man kind of slip his arm around the boy's shoulders as though he knew him and liked him a lot—the way my dad does me sometimes. Maybe it was his dad.

As I said, the quartet was singing "I Won't Have to Cross Jordan Alone," and that had reminded me of the Rio Grande and of the boy in our trunk. When I looked around and saw him, I realized that he had either snitched a ride with somebody else or he had done what thousands of other Mexicans do—waded or swum or been rowed across the river.

Seeing that interesting little guy, I almost forgot what else was going on around me. I nudged Poetry in his side and jerked my thumb in the direction of the boy.

Poetry looked and saw and let out an exclamatory whistle, which he shouldn't have done.

I noticed that there was a worried expression on the man's face and that he began whispering something to the boy, the way a boy's father does when a boy has done something he shouldn't have or maybe when the father thinks he has. Then the man raised his finger to his lips, which meant "Keep still," and he went on paying attention to what was going on on the platform.

Right that second the quartet finished, and a middle-aged minister, who had a forehead that reached all the way back to the back of his head, stood up and in a very kind voice asked if there were any people here who knew in their hearts that nothing could save a person from his sins except the Savior Himself.

"If there is anyone here who knows that and wants to trust Christ alone for his salvation, will he please raise his right hand?"

I noticed that several hands went up.

Then the minister asked all of us to shut our eyes and bow our heads, which we did, while he prayed a very nice, friendly prayer asking God to bless all the people who had raised their hands.

A little later we all stood up, and anybody who wanted to become a Christian that very night was supposed to go forward and into a small, friendly-looking canvas room beside the platform.

And as I watched, what should happen but the man the boy had been sitting beside stepped out into the aisle and was about the third or fourth one to go down to the front. There a Mexican minister quickly stepped off the platform to meet him, shook hands with him, and walked with him into the inquiry room.

I looked around out of the corner of my eye to see what different ones of the gang were thinking. Dragonfly was looking across the tent to where his parents were, and I noticed he swallowed kind of hard several times as though there might be tears trying to get into his eyes from somewhere. He was trying to keep them from doing it by swallowing, as people do in meetings like that.

Then I did get the surprise of my life. There was a rustling movement over where our folks were, and all of a sudden two women—one of them dressed in a new toast-colored suit with a green, flowered hat and the other, Dragonfly's mother—stepped out into the aisle.

Mom had her hand on Dragonfly's mom's arm, as though they were good friends, which they were anyway, and both of them went down to the front and into the little room.

I knew that my mother was already born again, so she couldn't be going down there to become a Christian herself. But I didn't get to wonder any farther, because right that second I heard a boy sniffling on the other side of Poetry, and I knew it was Dragonfly. I also knew it wasn't because he was allergic to anything.

Then I heard a sort of sob coming from his throat as he sniffled again and muttered in a gulping voice, "That's my mother. She's going to get saved."

Before you could say Jack Robinson, Dragonfly squeezed past Poetry and me and out into the aisle. Then he shot like a spindle-legged arrow straight for the open canvas door of the inquiry room to be with his mother.

I felt myself fighting tears. But I also felt wonderful inside, because I knew Dragonfly was going to have a saved mother. I was glad Mom knew how to pray and that she knew just what Bible verses to show Mrs. Gilbert so she could accept the Savior. I also knew Mom had a Bible in her handbag, which she always carried with her even when the handbag was already stuffed with everything you could think of.

I wondered for a minute if I ought to go down too, just to be with Dragonfly and let him know I was glad for him, but I waited awhile.

Then I got another surprise. And this time

it was the little Mexican boy who went hurrying down the outside aisle!

Little Jim, in the row in front of me, made a dive after him. Then Poetry and I and nearly all the Sugar Creek Gang went too, not to be saved again—you don't have to do that if you are *already* saved—but mostly because we wanted to be there when Dragonfly's mom became a Christian.

Well, it was really great. Maybe twenty people were saved that night before the meeting was over. I guess I never saw any prettier sight in my life than all those people in that friendly little tent room, giving their hearts to God.

Something inside of me felt like a Sugar Creek song—not the kind people sing in church but something like the friendly noise that Sugar Creek itself makes when the water from the spring tumbles into it. All these people with happy tears in their eyes made me think of that. I felt as good as I do when I see a fiery red cardinal winging across a sunshiny sky from one tree to another. For some reason it seemed as if God, who could make such wonderful things as Sugar Creek and redbirds for a boy to enjoy, was turning loose a whole flock of cardinals to fly around in people's hearts.

About the really prettiest sight I ever saw, though, was when Dragonfly's dad and my dad came in, too, and very quietly knelt down beside our two moms.

Dragonfly himself, who had been kneeling beside his mom, seemed a lot smaller than he was. He also seemed to want to get a little nearer to what was going on, so he snuggled in still closer and tucked his head beneath her arm and pushed the side of his face up close to hers as though he wanted to be there for protection.

I was afraid that by being so close to my mom he might get a whiff of her face powder and start a sneezing spell, but he didn't.

Well, while we were in the middle of all that gladness, Dad's little twenty-five-cent boy and his dad disappeared. One minute they were kneeling with the Mexican minister over in a corner, and the next minute they were gone.

Poetry, who was beside me, noticed first. He nudged his elbow into my ribs and whispered against my left cheek, "Hey, Bill! There goes our adventure! Let's go after it, or it will be gone forever!"

When Poetry whispered that, I quick opened my eyes in the direction my mind told me to, just in time to see the boy's bare foot disappearing under the tent flap, which meant that he had crawled out. The man himself was already gone.

6

Well, it certainly wasn't the right time and not a very dignified way to leave a gospel meeting, but I almost *had* to follow Poetry. So in a few seconds we were both outside the tent.

"There they go," Poetry exclaimed in an excited whisper.

My eyes and ears took in a quick circle of things there in the moonlight, such as a lot of palm trees with their husky, rusty, rasping leaves, a small garage with a tile roof, and behind it the dark beginning of an orange or grapefruit grove. Then I spied the man and the boy as they shot out from behind the garage and made a moonlit dash for the grove.

The next thing I knew, I was following Poetry as fast as he could go, right after them.

It was a silly thing to do, I suppose, but I kept on running behind and then beside Poetry deeper and deeper into that grapefruit grove, which was the kind of orchard it turned out to be.

I found that out when I stepped on something large and round about the size of a croquet ball. I stumbled and fell sprawling onto the dusty, cultivated ground. I also fell on several other grapefruit, one of which broke and squished its juice out and up and into my freckled face.

Poetry stooped, caught hold of me, and with a grunt got me to my feet.

"We're crazy to be doing this," I said. "How do we know which way they went? Besides we might get lost—oh!" I groaned as a brand-new pain shot through my right foot, the one the grapefruit had been under when I stepped on it.

But it's never easy to stop Poetry from doing anything exciting he has set his mind on doing. "I'll bet they're both illegals," he said. "Let's find out where they go and report to the police."

I was astonished to hear him say that. I knew from what Dad had told me that there were thousands of illegal immigrants in the United States helping harvest the oranges, grapefruit, lemons, sugar beets, cabbage, lettuce, carrots, and stuff. Besides, I had also heard Dad say, "That is a problem for the Mexican and United States government to solve." So even though I enjoyed a dangerous mystery as well as Poetry did, I certainly didn't like the idea of doing anything to harm that little twenty-five-cent guy, who, in the trunk of our car that afternoon, had looked as scared and lonesome as a little stray dog that nobody wanted.

So I answered Poetry by saying, "It's none of our business. Let's go back to the tent before we get lost"—which, after a one-sided argument, we decided to do.

Poetry started back in one direction, and I

started back in the other. Each one of us got stopped by the other's voice.

"The tent's *this* way," I exclaimed, surprised at his not knowing which way to go.

"It isn't, either. It's *this* way."

"It is not," I argued back.

We stayed stopped and looked at each other's worried moonlit faces, and—well, there we were! Every direction we looked, there were grapefruit trees, all of them the same size. Every direction looked like every other direction. The moon was too straight overhead for us to tell directions by it. Besides, when we left the tent we had run in every direction there is, so it looked as if we were really lost.

Anyway, Poetry was lost, and I didn't know for sure which way to go—not quite for sure anyway.

How long we might have stayed lost, I don't know, but pretty soon Poetry said, "Listen. I hear music. They're singing in the tent again."

I listened and heard music myself. Somebody was singing a solo. So we started in the direction of the music, glad we now knew which way to go to get back to the gang before they missed us and before two of our chaperons started worrying about us and wondering, *What on earth?* and, *Where?*

I felt pretty good when my sense of hearing told me the music was coming from the same direction as my mind had told me to go in the first place.

"How come they moved the tent over on

that side of the orchard?" Poetry asked, hating to admit how right I had been or maybe hating to admit how wrong *he* had been.

"Yeah, how come?" I said with a little mischievous sarcasm in my voice.

We hurried on toward the music. I was puzzled, though, when two or three minutes later the music told me we were almost there but there wasn't any tent or any electric light.

Poetry grabbed my arm and stopped me stock-still. *"Sh!"* he whispered and pulled me behind a grapefruit tree.

The mystery in his voice and the way he was grasping my arm scattered a shower of shivers all over me. We were within maybe ten yards of the music, which I noticed, when we stopped, was a man's voice with a guitar accompaniment. It seemed the music was coming from an old tin-roofed shed of some kind.

What on earth? I thought as the shower of shivers was still falling on me. I realized that our adventure had come to life again. The tree we were hiding behind was at the very edge of the grove. We had either gone all the way through, or else we had come out on a different side from the one the tent was on.

The old shed, which sat in a little clearing, had a banana plant growing on one side of its open door, and some kind of sweet-smelling, flowering vine was sprawled all over a heart-shaped trellis on the other side. For a second I was glad Dragonfly wasn't there to interrupt our silence with one of his fuzzy sneezes.

There wasn't even a light in the old shed, so the door was a big, black rectangular hole. At first I was sure the music was coming from inside, but I soon found out that it wasn't.

Right that second Poetry put his lips up close to my ear and whispered, "There's somebody hiding behind the trunk of that palm tree."

I looked toward the palm, which was about twenty feet from the shed, and saw the shadow of a man there. I also saw a quick rhythmic movement like the movement a person's wrist makes when he is strumming a guitar or a ukulele.

"What do you suppose is going on?" Poetry asked.

But I couldn't even guess. That is, I couldn't at first, but a moment later I saw a light in the shed. Somebody had struck a match, and quick as a flash the whole inside of the room was alive with light from what looked like a kerosene lamp just like the one we used in our upstairs at home.

Why, the old shed wasn't a shed at all, I thought. It was somebody's house—maybe the house of a Spanish American or even an illegal's house! The room I was looking into was about the size of our living room at home.

Then an interesting thing happened. A woman with sparkling jewels in her black hair lit another match, carried it over to the wall across the room, and lit a candle, which was standing on a table. The flickering light from the candle lit up something that was hanging on the wall. It looked like a—it *was!* It was a crucifix as big as a boy. A crucifix, as you maybe know, is a figure of the Savior fixed to a cross.

Then I saw the woman drop down on her knees and look up to the crucifix for a while as if she was talking to it with her mind. While she was doing that, the music outside stopped and everything was very quiet. Then the woman with the jewels in her hair got up, left the candle burning, and came and stood in the doorway. She called in a low, musical voice something in both Spanish and English, and the English was: "You sing very beautifully, Pedro."

She came out then and walked over to a bench beside the palm tree. The man with the guitar came from behind the tree trunk, and they sat down on the long bench together, one on one end and the other on the opposite end, and the man began to play and sing again.

It looked as if even though our adventure had come to life, the kind of life it had come to wasn't any of two boys' business, so I whispered to Poetry, "Let's get out of here."

"Yeah," he said in a disgusted tone of voice, "let's. That's probably a Mexican singing for his sweetheart"—which Dad says is what some Mexican senors do when they court their senoritas (a senor being a man and a senorita being a lady of some age or other, who for some reason isn't married yet).

Pretty soon, between the senor's verses, we heard some different music coming from farther away, and this time it was a lot of people singing a *hymn!*

Poetry and I started out as fast as we could go, both of us in the same direction this time, toward the new music, and we got back to the tent just in time to see and hear the boy evangelist dismiss the service. It was also in time to stop at least two of our chaperons from starting to worry about us.

We had had a queer adventure, but I was disappointed because we had lost our twenty-five-cent boy. If only we could find out where he and his dad had gone—if he *was* his dad. I felt as bad as Mom does sometimes when she loses her glasses and Dad and I have to stop doing whatever we are doing and help her look for them until she finds them again, right where she had thought they were in the first place.

But really, I needn't have felt so bad about our adventure being a flop, because it certainly wasn't over yet. You see, when Poetry is with us, he being the kind of boy he is, whenever there is anything that even looks like it might have an adventure in it, he always wants to investigate, and sometimes we run *ker-smack* into one when there wouldn't have been any at all.

As I said, I needn't have worried, because we did see Dad's twenty-five-cent Mexican boy again.

If I can, I will get going on that very exciting part of this story for you in the next chapter of this book.

7

Next day we drove to Old Point Lighthouse at Port Isabel, but we couldn't get in because it had been closed for years and locked. Then we went fishing off the jetties in Laguna Madre in the Gulf of Mexico near Padre Island. Some of the water in the Gulf, a few drops of it anyway, used to be up in Sugar Creek, we decided, and we had probably gone swimming in it. But I guess the fish in the Gulf didn't know the difference.

Anyway, they didn't want to bite. The wind was blowing hard, and the waves were high, and it was the lonesomest-looking place I'd ever been in. Not a one of us even got a bite except Big Jim, who landed two anemic-looking catfish that weren't any longer than from his wrist to his elbow. About all we got out of that day was a good launch ride; the name of the launch was *Gulf Pirate*.

Our guide for the day was the boy evangelist's friendly father, who drove us all around the country in his van. The boy evangelist went along. It was very interesting to discover that he was also a human being who enjoyed having fun as much as if he was an ordinary boy or a member of the Sugar Creek Gang. He and his dad had brought with them some gospel tracts and invitations to the tent meetings, which they distributed everywhere we went.

It was a good idea, we thought, so at Port Isabel the gang scattered itself all over the town, passing out tracts in all the stores to nearly everybody we saw.

"Where's that fish as big as a boy you were bragging about?" Poetry asked me that afternoon as he and I, side by side, went into and out of stores in a town called Mercedes, handing out pamphlets and invitations to the tent meetings.

"What fish as big as what boy?" I said, defending myself with an indifferent tone of voice.

Saying it, I thought how much more fun it would have been fishing with a dead bamboo pole and landing a six-inch-long chub out of the riffle just below our Sugar Creek swimming hole. At least a guy could get a *bite* in Sugar Creek, anyhow.

Before we went back to the hotel where our chaperons would be waiting for us to eat supper, we drove out to see a place called "The Cat," which was the absolutely most interesting and most sad-looking place I ever saw. "The Cat" was about forty houses, made out of sticks and pieces of tin and palm branches and woven willows. The whole place was about as big as the three-acre plot below the pignut trees on our farm.

A dozen bashful-acting, half-dressed Mexican boys and girls stopped playing in their grassless yards and stared at us.

But I guess they must have known the boy evangelist and his dad, because the minute his father stepped out of the car with a handful of tracts rolled in red paper—making them look like a handful of stick candy—the children came running from every direction. We helped pass out maybe a hundred Spanish gospel tracts.

While driving on to the hotel, Poetry, who was seated beside me in the middle seat of the van, said, "What's that song you're whistling, Bill?"

"What song?" I asked and pulled my thoughts back from "The Cat," where they had been, and fastened them onto the tune that had been galloping around in my mind when I didn't even know it. The song was "I Will Make You Fishers of Men." I was surprised to find out what it was, and for just a second I thought about what a funny thing a boy's mind is. He could be thinking about "The Cat" and riding in a van and at the same time be whistling a song and not even know that he was whistling it.

Well, the days flew by too fast. Almost before we realized it, there were only two days of vacation left. Our chaperons had been having a wonderful time, they said, just sitting around in the sun in their hotel patios, and the gang had been doing different things that boys like to do. We even borrowed and read some books from the public library, which was in a basement room under the bandstand in the park across from the hotel.

Our adventure would have to hurry up and

come to life again, I thought, or we would have to go back to Sugar Creek without knowing how it would have ended. Since I didn't have any fish as big as a boy to talk about, it would be hard to take all the kidding that the people would give me.

Dad, who had been reading the news, found out that the coal miners' strike was over, so we didn't have any excuse for not going back home to the ten-below-zero weather they were having up there and to the seventeen boy-battered desks in our one-room, red brick schoolhouse, which would have to have a roaring coal fire in its Poetry-shaped iron stove. The kids who sat up close to the stove would be smothering, and the ones in the back of the room would be able to see the frost in the air every time they exhaled.

We'd soon all be suffering our way through arithmetic and history and also geography. I knew that every time I looked at a map of the United States, my eyes would drop down to the bottom of it to the Mexican border, and I would wish summer would hurry up and come to Sugar Creek. I decided that I liked summer in the summertime at Sugar Creek better than I liked summer in the winter on the Mexican border.

Poetry and I were seated on the glider on our over-the-garage apartment porch when all of a sudden he, who had been reading the *Rio Grande Valley News,* gasped and said, "Hey, Bill, look, will you?"

First my eyes took in a wide circle all around

our porch. I noticed that not a one of the rest of the gang was there. They were down on the lawn tossing a softball around and making a lot of boy noise.

Then I looked at the headline Poetry's forefinger was pointing to, and it said:

Illegal Migration Costly in Lives and Money

"It's a shame to let all that excitement go on without our gang getting mixed up in it," Poetry said.

"I don't think it's fair myself. Hey!" I exclaimed. "What—"

The softball Circus had just thrown to Little Jim down by the palm tree struck the top of Little Jim's glove, glanced off and up, and hit the side of my head, which I had been resting against the screen. It startled me out of what few wits I had.

"Watch your step down there," I yelled down to the gang, and Circus called back, "That wasn't a *step*—that was a softball hitting a soft head," which I didn't think was very funny.

"Hey, you guys," Big Jim called up to Poetry and me. "The van is stopping out in front. We're going on another drive!"

"Who wants to go on a dumb drive?" I called back.

What I really wanted to do was to find out where the illegal had been killed last night and go and see the place myself. As I said, it didn't seem right for there to be so much adventurous excitement going on so close by and the Sugar Creek Gang not having a chance to get into the middle of it. It's like when a whirlwind starts moving across one of our fields back home—I always stop whatever I am doing and race out to it and try to run in the middle of it wherever it goes.

I told Poetry what I thought, but he answered, "It's too far—way up the Rio Grande near a little town called Roma. Besides, you might get your head bashed in."

"It might be safer than staying around *here*," I said, feeling the side of my head where the ball had struck it.

Our four chaperons had gone to Brownsville that day, where two of them were going to do some exciting shopping in some exciting shops to get a lot of useless trinkets to stand on our mantels and window ledges at home. Also they had promised a lot of other Sugar Creek mothers they'd bring back something for them. So the boy evangelist's father was taking care of us—even though not a one of us needed taking care of. He was going to drive us to a park where we would cook our own supper in Indian style on a sandy beach along the Rio Grande.

So far I had only seen the Rio Grande on a map and from a high bridge while we were crossing it. Of course, I had seen some of its brown water flowing through irrigation ditches, but today, our next to the last day in the valley, we were going to see it close up.

8

After we had left the main highway, we drove for what seemed miles and miles over dusty, narrow roads and through the dusty brush, which I later found out was made up of prickly pear cactus, bald cypress, horse chestnut, cottonwood poplar, ebony, burr oak, *huisache,* and what is called honey mesquite. There were also a lot of fierce-looking cacti called Spanish bayonet, but most of the cacti were prickly pear cactus, which the Indians feed to their cattle after they have cut off all the prickly parts.

After quite a long while we came to a little clearing, and there in front of our eyes was the wide, muddy river. It was bordered with different kinds of willows, which I found out later were mostly sandbar and black and buttonbush willow. Some of the buttonbush willows were growing in the water close to the shore.

For a while Circus seemed kind of glum. Even though there were plenty of trees, they were all different from the kinds that grew at Sugar Creek. Hardly a one of us felt at home. In fact, I felt almost as bashful in that park with all those strange trees standing around staring at us as I do when we have company at our house. A lot of the trees had thorns on them, which meant we couldn't climb them or play games in them. Besides, they were too dusty. We would get our clothes all dirty if we did.

But we did have a lot of fun. We didn't expect to be left alone all to ourselves, but the boy evangelist's father had to drive back to town to do some shopping and to broadcast a special program advertising the tent meetings. He planned to be back in time to have supper with us and drive us all back to the tent.

Not a one of us thought about running into any danger, because, after all, we were in what was called a public park. I say it was called that. If it had been a Sugar Creek park, there would have been dozens and dozens of people around and cars and picnic baskets and a lot of kids yelling and playing, and you wouldn't have to make your own excitement to be having a good time.

"I should be back around six o'clock for supper, but don't wait for me if I'm a little late. I'll be back in plenty of time to get you to the meeting tonight," the boy evangelist's father said. "You have everything you need, Big Jim?"

Our fuzzy-mustached leader nodded his head yes.

We did have everything we needed for a real Indian supper. There wouldn't be any danger of a brushfire, because we were going to build our fire on the beach itself, where the only thing that could burn would be what we ourselves carried there.

We had had Indian suppers before, especially when we were on our camping trips in the summertime in the Far North of the United States—but you know all about that if you have read our exciting experiences in the book called *Screams in the Night*.

Right away we dug our eighteen-inch-square hole in the ground, far enough up on the beach so that there wouldn't be any Rio Grande water seeping into the bottom of it. We lined it with stones and then filled it with kindling wood and sticks. We piled other pieces of wood on top until the pile was about two feet high.

Then Big Jim started the fire. We let it burn for a whole hour, feeding it with dry wood to keep a very hot fire all that time. At the end of the hour we scooped out all the ashes and live coals, leaving the lining of terribly hot stones. Then we lined the whole hot hole with green leaves, mixing in a few lettuce leaves, which Big Jim had brought along on purpose.

As quick then as Mom could have done it herself, Big Jim laid in a big slice of steak apiece for each member of the gang and one for the boy evangelist's dad. He also put in some potatoes and corn on the cob and carrots (which almost none of the gang liked but had to eat to keep our parents happy; besides, carrots are supposed to be good for us, and maybe they are).

On top of that we put on more leaves, piled more stones on top of the leaves, and then spread on a couple of soaking wet burlap sacks.

It was enough to make a nice little mound like a small grave in a cemetery.

After about two hours, our supper would be all cooked by the terribly hot steam from the hot rocks and the wet burlap sacks.

While we were waiting, we played different games and told stories. It was fun imagining ourselves to be pirates who had sailed in from the Gulf of Mexico and up the Rio Grande to bury our treasure there.

We even played illegals and robbers, some of us filling our pockets with small stones representing money that we had earned in the States picking grapefruit or pulling carrots and stuff. The rest of the gang would hide in the willows down by the river to waylay us. Somebody would yell, "OK, gang, it's dark now! It's time for the illegals to come out of the brush and get their backs wet swimming the river!"

Only, of course, we didn't even get our *feet* wet. That river was such a big, wide, unfriendly thing that any boy would be silly to wade out into it. It certainly was different from Sugar Creek, where we knew every inch of the bottom for a mile each side of the spring. We knew where every big rock was and every little riffle and every stepoff. We even knew the names of some of the big bass that hid out in the deep water below the Sugar Creek bridge and nobody had caught yet.

It gave me the creeps to imagine myself taking even a few steps out into that big coldhearted Rio Grande. Besides, it certainly wouldn't be safe.

Well, time flew by fast, yet hardly fast enough for me, because I was hungry even before we buried our uncooked dinner in the ground.

"OK, illegal," Poetry said to me when he and I were alone and close to the water's edge. He quick stooped, scooped up a handful of the Rio Grande, and splashed some of it on my shoulders. "Let's go hide in the brush up there on that hill."

"Stop it," I exclaimed. I swung around and grabbed up a handful of water myself and made a "wet*face*" out of him.

But it was innocent fun and nobody let himself get mad, which is silly for a boy to do when he is playing any kind of a game.

"Look," all of a sudden Poetry said, "see that black log over there across the river on the Mexican side?"

I looked across the unfriendly river toward the gray-and-brown hills on the other side, and sure enough there was a big black log. "What about it?" I said.

"It's too black for a log. You know what that looks like?"

"No, what?"

"It looks like an inflated rubber life raft. I'll bet somebody uses it for a boat. Somebody maybe gets paid for taking illegals back and forth."

I wished I had my binoculars, but of course I didn't.

"Don't tell Dragonfly it's a rubber boat,"

Poetry said mischievously, "or he will be allergic to it and start sneezing."

Right that second, from somewhere behind me, Dragonfly did sneeze, but it was because a little whirlwind of dust had come spiraling out of the brush and was heading across the beach toward the river.

"Hey!" I yelled at the whirlwind, starting toward it on the run. "Don't you *dare* cross that river. You can't carry all that dust across into Mexico without permission."

By the time I had said that, I was right in the center of the whirling dust and leaves and stuff that the whirlwind was stealing from Texas and was trying to take across into Mexico without paying duty on it.

Pretty soon it would be time to take our steak supper out of our hot-rock cooking utensil. The van still hadn't come, but when six-thirty came, Big Jim said, "OK, gang, come and get it."

It took only a few minutes to get the sand off the steaming burlap sacks, the top layer of stones off the leaves, and the leaves off the yummiest supper a boy ever cooked without a mother to worry about all the dirt he might accidentally eat.

After supper, when it began to get dark and still no van came, we started to look at each other's half-worried faces and to wonder how long we'd have to wait. It was about the lonesomest park I'd ever seen. Not a single other human had showed up all afternoon, and we'd not even heard the sound of a car.

The sun had already set, and even though the afterglow was a very pretty pink and purple and gold, for some reason I didn't seem to enjoy it.

"Are there any wild animals down here?" Little Jim asked from within two inches of me, where he sat crowded up close.

Not a one of us seemed to want to answer him, because the answer would probably be yes, and we didn't want to say out loud what our thoughts were already screaming at our minds.

In what seemed a very short time it was dark, and it wasn't any nice, friendly dark, either, as it is up North along the creek. There weren't any bullfrogs bellowing bass solos in the riffles, or any big night herons crying, "Quok-quok!" as they flew up the bayou, or any splashing of a big bass feeding in the lily pads, or any husky, rusty rustle of the blades of the corn. There wasn't even the rasping of palm tree leaves, because this wasn't any civilized park but one with only the native trees and bushes and shrubs of Texas growing in it.

"We'd better get a fire started," Big Jim said, "so when he comes for us, or if he sends somebody else after us, they will see the light and know where we are."

We brought it to a vote as to whether to try to follow one of the many crisscrossing dusty roads back through the brush to the highway— and thus run the risk of getting lost—or start a fire and stay by the river and wait. The vote was six to nothing in favor of staying where we were.

It certainly wasn't comfortable feeling all alone in the lonely dark. The river flowing through the buttonbush willows sounded like the hissing of a snake, and when we did hear sounds in the brush behind us, there wasn't a single sound I knew. It seemed we were not only at the bottom of Texas but also at the very end of the world.

9

The end of the world!

Of course, it wasn't that, but when you are alone in a strange, wild country where law-breakers hang out, and it is night, and your mind won't quit imagining all kinds of things that *might* happen—even when you've been *wanting* an exciting adventure, you wish that whatever is going to happen will hurry up and do it, no matter how dangerous it is. You also half hope it *won't*.

I guess one reason I was worrying was because I figured my folks were doing it back at the hotel, if they were home yet from Brownsville —or maybe by this time they were in the tent, wondering why we weren't there too.

"Maybe Mr. Mulder had a flat tire," Big Jim said casually, and I could tell he was trying to keep us calm by using a calm voice. "That rocky road leading into this wilderness is enough to give any tire a stone bruise or a blowout."

Big Jim decided to start the fire right away because, as he said, "If there *are* any wild animals around here, it will keep them away."

"*Wild animals!*" Dragonfly exclaimed in a frightened voice. "Where?"

"I said '*if* there are,'" Big Jim answered. But his tone of voice still sounded as though he was trying to keep the youngest ones of us from being even more scared than we were. Then he yawned the way he does when he is trying to be indifferent and started making a little wigwam of wood, using that which we had left over from our afternoon fire.

Just then Dragonfly said, "*Psst!* Listen! I hear something coming!"

I was used to hearing him hiss like that. It generally didn't mean a thing—nothing very important, anyway, although sometimes it did. But when he hissed like that right in the middle of our tense huddle, it made me feel nervous.

We strained our eyes and ears in different directions. At first I didn't hear anything at all.

Then Circus said, "It's somebody coming across the river."

I looked quick out over the shimmering waves of the Rio Grande, expecting to see somebody wading or swimming across. And actually, honest-to-goodness-for-sure, somebody *was* coming! I could see a long black shadow right out in the moonlit middle of the river.

"It's the rubber life raft," Poetry said.

I guess we all saw it at about the same time. And all the frightening things I had ever heard or read about illegals and trouble on the Mexican border—such as thirty-eight bodies being found in the river, the new migration, and the murder at Roma only yesterday—all those things came swarming into my mind like a half-dozen bumblebees at Sugar Creek when I accidentally poke a stick into their nest.

Big Jim quickly stopped starting a fire.

To move from where we were or not to move was the question. We could scramble up the bank into the brush and hide, but who wanted to get scratched up with cactus or mesquite or cat's claw, or run the risk of getting hurt by a wild animal or something? So we hid ourselves as well as we could behind the nearby buttonbush willows.

It seemed we were all so scared we couldn't move, and all the time, fast second after fast second, the black boat was coming nearer to our beach. I could already hear the splashing of oars in the water.

"Anybody see how many there are in the boat?" Big Jim asked.

"Looks like only one," Dragonfly said, and it did.

"'S'matter? You cold?" I asked Little Jim, who was shivering against my shivering arm.

He didn't answer for a second, but he did press a little closer. Then he astonished me by having a sense of humor right in the middle of that danger. He said, "I'm getting up close to you so you won't be s-scared!"

"If there's only *one* in the boat," Big Jim said, "then he isn't bringing any illegals over from Mexico. He's coming over here to take some *back* with him!"

Well, *that* sent another shower of scared shivers all over me.

Big Jim added, "That means that some-where behind us in the brush there is an immi-grant or two or more hiding, waiting until the boat gets here. Then they will dash down the bank, climb in, and be rowed back."

"See!" Poetry exclaimed. "He's rowing straight for us!"

I might have guessed he would. Of course he would want the boat to be protected from sight by some growth along the shore, and the buttonbush willows we were hiding in would be just right.

Nearer and nearer the boat came and also—it seemed—faster and faster.

Then a flashlight in the boat went on and off three times. A second or two later, there was an answer—three fast, fleeting flashes from the bank up the shore.

Poetry, on the other side of me from Little Jim, whispered, "Anybody want to play a game of illegals and robbers now?"

"It's the wrong time to be funny," Circus said.

And Big Jim cut in with a calm, low voice, "There isn't anything to be afraid of. We are getting a good education without having to study. In a minute we will see acted out in real life the things we have been reading about—immigrants being transported across the Rio Grande. In years to come we can tell about it to our children and our grandchildren."

Dragonfly interrupted him by saying, "If we live that long."

When the boat came to within twenty-five feet of the shore, all of a sudden it stopped coming nearer, and the lone man in it began rowing faster, up along the shore and around a little neck of land at the end of our beach.

"Maybe he saw us," Big Jim said.

We were all sitting there, wondering, *What next?* when all of a sudden, right in front of our eyes, *the boat was empty!* The river's current had caught it and whirled it about, and it was floating back downstream with nobody in it. One minute the man had been in the boat, and the next he wasn't.

We hadn't seen him climb out—or even fall out. And now, instead of carrying the boat on past us downstream, it looked as if the current was pushing it toward the beach again. Next thing I knew, it had come to rest against the shore in a little cove not more than twenty-five yards from the buttonbush willows we were hiding in.

My eyes started chasing up and down the river to see where on earth whoever it was had gone.

"You think he fell out and drowned?" whispered Little Jim.

Poetry whispered back, "He might have seen or heard us and thought we were officers and got scared and jumped out and swam to shore—or maybe swam back toward the other shore, swimming under the water."

"But nobody saw him in the water," I said. "And he would have to come up for air sometime."

"Maybe somebody up there in the brush shot him with a gun that had a silencer on it," Poetry said, "and he just tumbled out."

It didn't seem possible that, with our twelve eyes watching the boat, not a one of us had seen what happened.

I turned the idea over in my mind. At the same time my mind itself seemed to be turning over and over.

Well, a gang of inquisitive boys couldn't be quiet too long, or they would get the heebie-jeebies, so Poetry said, "Let's send out a couple of spies to the boat to see what happened"—which meant that he was still halfway between playing a game and real life. Then he added, "Maybe he *did* get shot and just fell into the bottom of the boat, and that's why we can't see him."

Big Jim didn't like the idea of sending out spies. He said, "If somebody shot him, then the very minute any of us stepped out into the open, we'd probably get shot ourselves."

Only a second after that, things really started to happen. Quicker than a flash, from up the bank came running steps. A man and a boy darted out into the moonlight, dashed past our hiding place, and raced on to the boat.

"Our adventure again," Poetry hissed to me.

"Dad's twenty-five-cent boy," I said back to him.

Talk about brain-whirling excitement! Suddenly there were three people beside the boat instead of two. The third one rose up from behind the boat with an oar in his hands. With a fast, fierce movement he raised the oar high and brought it down with a smash on the head of the other man, who let out a wild yell, threw up his arms, staggered backward, and slumped down into the sand at the edge of the water.

Before I could get my muddled brain to thinking, Dad's twenty-five-cent boy and the third man were in a fierce, one-sided fight, and I could hear grunts and socks and clothes tearing. I could also see the boy's fists flying faster than mine did that time I had my fierce fight up North with Shorty Long.

Any minute I expected the boy to get knocked flat, which he would have if the man's fist ever hit him just right.

"Let's rush out and help him," Circus said, saying what most of us probably thought.

But Big Jim stopped us, saying firmly, "No, not yet. That might be an arresting officer employed by the Mexican or the American government, whose business it is to stop illegal immigrants."

But then something else began to happen. There was the sound of more quick running steps, and I saw the little guy running across the sand straight toward our hideout. He got two-thirds of the way to us before the man caught up with him, grabbed him, and slammed him on his back to the ground. A second later the man was on top of him, holding him down and saying a lot of angry-sounding Spanish words!

Talk about anybody's temper getting ready to explode! Mine was like a lighted firecracker with a very short sputtering fuse. I wanted to see the boy get away because I was not only sure the savage man was a robber, but my sense of fair play made me want to see the man get the living daylights knocked out of him. I also had a lightning-flash mental picture of that little guy down on his knees in the tent, giving his heart to God.

Along with my ready-to-explode temper there was a warm love for the little guy. It wasn't any of my business whether he was an illegal immigrant or not, but it was my business to do something to help keep a human being from getting hurt by a big bully.

The man kept on yelling down into the boy's face some terribly fast Spanish words that sounded as if he was swearing at him.

Well, if there is anything that makes me sadder in my heart than anything else, it's to hear a person use the Savior's name or the heavenly Father's name that way. I wondered quick what Little Jim was thinking. I knew swearing not only made him feel sad, but it also blew up his small temper till it was as big as a balloon at a county fair.

As you maybe know, Big Jim understood a little Spanish, so when he said to us, "He's swearing," that was too much for Little Jim.

And that's how our whole gang got mixed up in the fight. We had to get into it—or let Little Jim get the living daylights knocked out of *him*.

Almost the very second Big Jim told us the man was swearing, Little Jim was gone from beside me. I saw a streak of moonlit curly-haired boy shooting out from the shade of our willows across the sand and making a flying-tiger leap straight for the back of the bully. He got there only about five seconds before five other boys did.

What a scramble. That really was one. Our battle with that fierce-fighting wild man was something. I say *wild* because, when six boys landed on him from about six different directions at the same time, he started acting like a man that had suddenly gone crazy or like a chicken that has just had its head cut off.

I didn't know much of anything for a while —a boy doesn't when he is excited or mad and in a fight. But I did sort of realize three things: one was that our robber wasn't an American, because he was swearing in Spanish; also he was all wet, which meant he had slipped out of the boat when it was still in the river and had swum along behind it, pushing it to shore, making it look as if there wasn't anybody in it at all; and third, he was as strong as an ox.

If we hadn't been a husky gang of boys, we could have all been badly hurt. For a half second I even thought I was glad my parents had made me hoe potatoes and do all kinds of other hard farm work, because when I got my arm around the man's wet leg, I shut my eyes and gritted my teeth and held on like a bulldog. Circus had a hold on his other leg; and Big Jim, Poetry, Little Jim, and Dragonfly were doing other things to the rest of him. Also the minute he could, Dad's twenty-five-cent boy scrambled to his feet and helped us hold the man down.

"Get me one of the gunnysacks, Bill," Big Jim ordered me.

"Why?" I asked.

I could tell that already Big Jim was feeling fine. He said mischievously, "To put our fish in. Didn't you say you were going to catch a fish as big as a boy? Well, here's one as big as a man."

I was back in a whiz with the gunnysack.

"Now," Big Jim said, panting and holding onto the man's arm, "get the fishing line out of my hip pocket."

In only a minute or two we had the man's feet shoved into the gunnysack and Big Jim's fishing line wrapped round and round his ankles.

Almost the second we finished tying his legs, a car swung onto the shore above us, and a spotlight lit up the whole beach.

And then the most astonishing thing happened. The light hadn't any sooner focused on our tangled-up scramble than our little Mexican boy took one frightened, eye-blinking look at it, jumped like a scared rabbit, whirled around, and dashed for the river. He plunged in and splashed his way out through the shallow water until it was too deep for him to wade any farther. Then he began a fierce, fast swim toward Mexico.

10

Crazy things were really going on on the Mexican border that night. The story the Sugar Creek Gang could tell to their grandchildren was going to be very exciting as well as very interesting. The only thing was, if we told it to our grandchildren at night as a bedtime story, they wouldn't want us to stop in the middle but would cry for more. And if we kept on till we got to the end, it'd be too late for the littlest ones to stay up.

I could very easily imagine myself being a grandfather with a couple of wriggling, squirming grandchildren on my lap and maybe one of them using my long, thick reddish whiskers for a pillow.

Well, there we were—six panting boys holding a wild man down on his stomach on a sandy beach along the Rio Grande. A bright spotlight from somebody's car was shining on us. Another man with a hurt head was lying up the beach from us, and the Mexican boy we had tried to rescue was swimming like mad toward his native land, crossing the Rio Grande alone.

That is, I thought he was going to have to cross it alone. For a second the spotlight swung away from us and focused on the swimming boy out in the river.

"Hey!" Poetry, whose eyes were looking where mine were, exclaimed. "There's another boat out there! He's climbing into it!"

My half-light-blinded eyes looked quick toward the place where the first boat had been, but it wasn't there.

Also gone was the man who ten or more minutes before had gotten his head socked with an oar and had been lying beside the boat. That could mean only one thing, and that was that the boy's dad (if he was his dad) had regained consciousness (if he had lost it) and still had strength enough to paddle the boat.

By the time my eyes could get back to the twenty-five-cent boy again, he was already in the boat and was helping row back to the other side.

All this time our prisoner was struggling fiercely, and we were still holding on for dear life. We knew we didn't dare let loose for a second. If he had a knife, as some criminals do have, he'd probably use it on us.

And then two men who had been in the car that had the spotlight were hurrying down the bank to our battlefield to take our prisoner off our hands.

In a minute the officers—which is what they were—were taking charge and doing the different things that arresting officers do, such as putting handcuffs on our prisoner and asking us a lot of questions and stuff.

They had us tell the whole story, which we did, using six different excited voices to do it. It turned out that we had caught one of the worst criminals Mexico had ever had. He had broken out of a jail named the Black Palace, in Mexico City. Both the United States government and the Mexican government had been looking for him. The only thing was, as soon as he gave up he didn't act like a vicious criminal at all. In fact, he didn't even look like one. He had a haircut and shave, and he answered questions in a polite voice. Also, he could talk English almost as well as Spanish.

"It's a wonder one of you boys didn't get slashed to pieces," the tallest officer said to us.

"Which one?" Dragonfly asked.

The shorter officer, whose face I could see pretty well in the moonlight, grinned and said to Dragonfly, "You, probably." Then he added, talking to our prisoner, "Well, Pedro, let's get started. You're going back to live in the Palace again. They've been missing your singing down there."

Pedro! Singing! Poetry and I gasped at the same time, and my imagination picked me up and carried me over the top of the mesquite and cottonwood poplar and bald cypress and prickly pear cactus to a grapefruit grove and a weather-scarred, tin-roofed house. I was seeing a black-haired senorita lighting a candle before a boy-sized crucifix, and a man with a guitar singing behind a palm tree.

Boy oh boy! Poetry and I had been a whole lot closer to a live adventure that night than we'd realized. Pedro had probably been following the twenty-five-cent boy and his dad that very night, trying to find out when they were going back to Mexico.

In the excitement of things, I had almost forgotten the boy and his dad—if it was his dad. I had even forgotten my own dad and our other three chaperons and the boy evangelist's dad, who still hadn't come for us.

But a little later, while we were still on the beach, the van came swinging down one of the park's dusty roads to where we were. All three dads were in it—the boy evangelist's, Dragon-fly's, and mine.

It took only a little while for them to explain why nobody had come sooner. The police had set up a roadblock at the park entrance, and no cars except police cars had been allowed to enter.

"It's this way," one of the officers explained. "We discovered that illegal immigrants were using rubber life rafts from army surplus stores. An illegal would row across the river, tie the boat to shore, and leave it for some other illegal to use for a return trip. Pedro, just out of jail, found out about that and was cashing in on it, and—well, you know the rest of what happened. Thanks to you boys, he tried it once too often."

And this has got to be the last part of this story, because nothing else happened that was very important until we got back home to Sugar Creek.

In the van on the way to town, Dragonfly,

who was sitting beside me in the middle seat, sneezed three times in fast succession—the first time I'd heard him sneeze that many times that fast for an hour or two.

"Don't start that again!" I said to him. "You haven't sneezed for over an hour. How come?"

Dragonfly giggled and said, "I guess I forgot. I can sneeze anytime I want to, though!"

"You cannot," Poetry challenged him.

"I can too," Dragonfly argued back.

"All right, then, let's hear you do it."

Dragonfly answered in a saucy voice, saying, "I'm sorry, but I don't happen to want to" —which was an old joke and was maybe a little bit funny.

Well, we'd had a wonderful vacation, and especially a wonderful next-to-the-last day, but I wasn't satisfied. Most every minute of the way to town, it seemed that my mind's eye was seeing the little Mexican boy swimming like fury out to a rubber boat, climbing in, and then helping the man row as fast as they could out across the moonlit Rio Grande to their own country. I didn't like the idea of having him swim out of my life like that. I might never get to see him again. He would probably never get to become a citizen of the United States.

Little Jim helped me feel better about it when he said, "Maybe if he and his dad were really saved in the tent that night, they'll hunt up a preacher in Mexico who knows how to be saved the way the Bible says, and they'll join his church."

I could tell by the tone of voice Little Jim was using that he was getting sleepy. He rested his head against my shoulder, sighed a heavy sigh, and kept still, which made me feel pretty fine. If there's anything a boy likes, it is to have a boy he likes like him back.

I felt fine for another reason too. After another day we would be leaving Texas and would be on our way back to Sugar Creek.

We hadn't caught any fish as big as a boy, but we had caught a fierce criminal, and by doing that we had maybe helped keep a lot of illegal immigrants from getting killed.

I was surprised when Poetry said from beside me, "What's that song you're whistling, Bill?"

"What song?" I asked and listened to my thoughts. I was whistling "I Won't Have to Cross Jordan Alone."

It was a good song. I knew I would never forget it as long as I lived. And because I was a Christian, I would probably remember it *after* I got through living. I might even sing it on my way to heaven.

During the week we had been in the Rio Grande Valley, we had heard the quartet sing that song nearly every night. So when somebody in the van started to sing it, the rest of us started to help him.

Maybe some of us sounded a little like Mom's hens singing in our barnyard. Poetry's changing voice actually did sound like the snoring croak of a middle-sized bullfrog, and mine didn't sound like anything.

Only Circus's was good, which it always is—maybe because he practices more than the rest of us. Sometimes he does it from the top branches of the elm sapling that grows along the bayou—right where the old rail fence starts its lazy climb up Strawberry Hill, on top of which is the abandoned cemetery, where Old Man Paddler's wife is buried, and where . . .

Hey! Did I ever tell you about the time the gang was coming home one dark night from fishing for catfish just above the Sugar Creek bridge, and on the way home we decided to pass close to the cemetery to convince ourselves we weren't afraid to—and just as we got there, we saw a lantern and somebody digging a hole behind a thicket of chokecherry shrubs?

I can't seem to remember telling you about that. So maybe my next story will be all about that mysterious adventure and the very strange-acting person who was digging there, and why.